THE MYSTERY OF
THE BACKLOT BANSHEE

Other titles in this series:
The Mystery of Microsneezia

Learning Company Books
A division of Riverdeep, Inc.
500 Redwood Boulevard, Novato, CA 94947, USA

Editor: Brenda Kienan
Illustrations: Animotion, Inc.
Cover design: Mez Design
Page layout: Creative Media Applications

This is a work of fiction. The characters, incidents, and dialogues are products of the author's imagination and are not to be construed as real. Any resemblance to persons living or dead, or to actual events, is entirely coincidental.

ISBN 0-7630-7620-1

First printing: March 2004
Printed in the United States of America

10 9 8 7 6 5 4 3 2 1

Visit Learning Company Books at
www.learningcompanybooks.com.

The publisher thanks Kenny Dinkin
for his creative contributions.

THE MYSTERY OF
THE BACKLOT BANSHEE

Ellen Weiss and Mel Friedman

Learning Company Books
A division of Riverdeep, Inc.

DAILY *Hollywood Star*

| More News Than You Can Use! | **WEATHER TODAY** If you have to ask, you're so not here. |

Casting Completed for Cliffhanger on Crowning Case of Clandestine Crime Fighter's Career

SPECIAL TO THE STAR

by Hedda Steeme

Casting on the long-awaited crime thriller The *Doomsday Worm* is almost completed, Boffo Pictures announced today. Megastar Jason Torch will play the leading role of Perry Boston, the true-life crime fighter. Shooting will begin when the perfect stunt double for Mr. Torch is found.

The big-budget picture, seven years in the making, is based on the last—and most famous—of Perry Boston's cases. Mr. Boston retired ten years ago to write a best-seller about his hair-raising adventures. The book, titled *Extreme Measures: The Life of a Daredevil Crime Fighter,* told the tale of Mr. Boston's amazing double life. By day he was a mild-mannered pencil-eraser manufacturer; by night he was the dreaded foe of all evildoers.

The Doomsday Worm focuses on Mr. Boston's pursuit and capture of genius computer hacker Morris Nogudnik.

Mr. Nogudnik was on the "ten most-wanted list" of the FBI, the CIA, the PTA, and the Overdue Book Squad of the Springfield, Ohio, Librarians Association.

"Jason Torch will make an absolutely fabulous Perry Boston," said Wilton Thumbling, the producer and director of the film. "He is a monster, monster talent."

Perry Boston is expected to work closely with Mr. Torch and his stunt double to make sure that their portrayals of him are accurate. Boffo Pictures also disclosed today that Vince DeGrotto, who starred as "Mr. Ugly" on TV's *The Losers,* will play the part of computer genius Morris Nogudnik.

SIREN-DIPPITY

Rrrrrippp!!

"Hey, guys! Look what I found! Is this serendipity or what?" Leslie Clark sat up sharply in her lounge chair by the edge of the Hoi Polloi Hotel's pear-shaped swimming pool. The hot Los Angeles sun was beating down on her neat poolside arrangement of lawn chairs, backpacks, grocery bags, and essential reading matter. As she shifted in her chair, three thick books and four different newspapers tumbled from her lap onto the ground. The pretty eleven-year-old, who loved to read and usually treated books with utmost respect, hardly noticed. She had torn an article from the front page of one of her newspapers and was waving it frantically in the air to catch her friends' attention.

Leslie and her friends were members of the ClueFinders team of kid detectives. The ClueFinders had just returned from Central America, where they had solved the mystery of the missing keys to the locks on the Panama Canal. They were in Los Angeles for a much-needed vacation before heading back home to San Francisco.

Owen Lam noticed Leslie's exaggerated motions first. He was practicing a difficult one-armed handstand on the nearby grass. "Siren-*whaaaat*?" he called out to Leslie. He jerked his head around to get a better view of the item Leslie was waving. That was a big mistake. As his head abruptly zigged, Owen's feet unfortunately zagged.

"Tim-BER, dudes!" Owen cried as he toppled over. He landed on two bulging food bags next to Leslie's chair.

Leslie instantly curled up into a tiny, protective ball. Then she relaxed slowly and shook out her long black curls. "Don't you know it's dangerous to practice gyroscopically unstable stunts like that?" she scolded.

Owen, who was also eleven years old, sat in a growing puddle of lemonade and scratched his head. Pulling a totaled peanut-butter-and-jelly sandwich out from under his sneakers, he said, "Hey, gimme a break. I'm still working on those first two words of yours—'siren-*whatsis*'."

Leslie looked at Owen's wet shorts, his grape-stained sneakers, and his hangdog expression. In spite of herself, she couldn't help laughing. "It's only one word, Owen—'serendipity'," she said. "It applies to situations in which you discover something happy or fortunate by accident—like this." She held up the torn newspaper page again.

Owen didn't notice. He was staring mournfully at the flattened sandwich. "I can't believe I put an inch of sneaker tread into a perfectly awesome sandwich. Oh, well," he sighed, "I guess we'll have to get some replacement food. It's a good thing there's still pizza in the world." He got up on his hands and knees and began rummaging in the grass.

"Looking for these?" Leslie asked. She leaned over and fetched a pair of purple sunglasses that had fallen between her books. Owen never went anywhere without his trademark shades.

"Excellent!" Owen said, his face brightening.

Just then two figures emerged from the water. Joni Savage, the twelve-year-old leader of the ClueFinders, had been teaching Santiago Rivera, the group's technical wizard, how to do a backstroke.

"What's going on?" asked Joni as she grabbed a towel from the back of her chair and dried herself off. "I couldn't see anything without my glasses, but I heard Owen yelling." She squeezed some water out of her thick, fiery-red braids.

Santiago, whose dark eyes missed nothing, quickly surveyed the disaster scene. "Wow!" he said. "It looks like a tornado ripped through our picnic bags."

"That was no tornado, that was Hurricane Owen," Leslie said.

Tiny streams of lemonade still ran down Owen's legs. "Sorry about the mess," Owen said. "I fell over doing a one-hander."

"What's the damage?" Joni asked.

The twelve-year-old Santiago peered into the exploded bags. "Hmm, it looks like almost everything inside is flattened," he said.

"Guess we can forget about our poolside picnic."

"No need," Joni said. "I packed extra sandwiches —just in case." She unzipped the largest compartment of her knapsack, revealing a large juice bottle, three boxes of cookies, and a stack of assorted sandwiches in plastic bags. "I think there's enough here for everyone—even Owen."

"Yesss!" Owen exclaimed, pumping his arm in joy.

"You know, Owen," Santiago said, cleaning up the food mess. "I don't know anyone who thinks more about eating than you."

"Me either," said Owen. "It's part of my charm."

"Hey, I almost forgot," Leslie interrupted, holding her torn page from the *Daily Hollywood Star* aloft for a third time. "I really think you guys ought to see this. I clipped it from today's paper. We can't afford to pass up this opportunity."

Joni set aside her turkey sandwich and took the newspaper article from Leslie. "What opportunity?" she asked. Then she put on her large round glasses and began to read the story aloud to the group. The moment she reached the names "Jason Torch" and "Perry Boston" she stopped.

"This is awesome!" she cried. "My favorite actor is going to play my favorite detective. When Santiago and I first started the ClueFinders, we read Perry Boston's book for tips on solving mysteries."

Santiago and Owen peered over Joni's shoulders to read the story. "Hey, it says they're shooting at Boffo Pictures," Santiago said. "Didn't we pass that on the way here?"

"Mmm-hmm," Leslie said. "As I recall, it is within easy walking distance of our hotel."

"Boy, I'd give anything to watch them filming," Santiago said.

"Me, too," Joni added. "But there's practically zero chance of that. Most shoots are closed to the public."

Suddenly Owen's face lit up. "I know how we can get in." He pointed to the advertisement at the end of the article. "Boffo is looking for a stunt double for Jason Torch."

"So?" said Santiago.

Owen beamed. "Check out the qualifications. The double must be fearless, good looking, an expert skateboarder, and able to eat lots of free pizza. Who does that remind you of?"

Santiago shrugged. "I give up—Heath Ledger?"

"O-W-E-N," Owen spelled out. He stood up straight and tall and made his best fearless, good-looking face. "Am I a shoo-in, dudes, or am I a shoo-in?"

"Be serious, Owen," Santiago objected. "You have straight black hair, and Jason Torch and Perry Boston are both blond."

"No, wait a minute, Santiago," Joni interjected. "Owen may be onto something. There's nobody better on a skateboard. And with a wig or some hair coloring he could pass for Jason Torch's double."

Santiago stared hard at Owen. "Hmm," he said, "you might be right."

Joni grinned. "If Owen doesn't get the job, at least we'll get in for his audition. Maybe we can sneak a peek at Jason Torch or even get Perry Boston's autograph."

"Owen, I take it back," Santiago said. "You are a genius."

Owen took a big bow. "Owen Einstein, at your service, dudes!"

"Now all we need to do is get Owen a blond stunt wig," Joni said. "When's the audition, again?"

"Friday morning," replied Santiago. "That's tomorrow, so we've got to move fast."

"I'll ask LapTrap to do a grid search for the nearest wig store," Joni said.

LapTrap was the only nonhuman member of the ClueFinders team. Originally developed by the government for military combat use, he proved too whiny and fearful under fire. So the military gave him to Joni's Uncle Horace, a scientist. Uncle Horace, in turn, donated LapTrap to the ClueFinders as their own personal supercomputer. LapTrap was the latest in a series of multifunctional T.U.R.T.L.E. flying superlaptops. The acronym T.U.R.T.L.E. stood for Turbo-charged Ultra Rugged Terrain Laptop Equipment.

"Where is LapTrap, anyway?" asked Leslie. "I haven't seen him all day."

"He's hiding out in our hotel room," Santiago said. "He was afraid to go near the water. He was scared he'd get his microprocessors wet."

"I think we might be able to coax him out," Joni said. "He's a big Perry Boston fan, too. He won't want to miss a chance to scan Perry Boston's autograph onto his hard drive."

"Hey, dudes," Owen interrupted, "enough talk. If we don't eat now, your ticket into Boffo Pictures—me—will go on strike."

The four friends laughed and dug into their picnic meal—this time in earnest.

Find the wig store closest to the ClueFinders' hotel.

CHAPTER 2

THE WAIL OF THE BANSHEE

Friday was shaping up to be another scorcher. The ClueFinders arrived at Boffo Pictures a few minutes early. Much to their surprise, a long line had already formed outside the studio gates. Above the entrance a large notice was posted:

AUDITIONS TODAY!

—— **Studio 43** ——

For Stunt Double for Jason Torch in
The Doomsday Worm

All applicants must take test on an OBSTACLE COURSE.

If you've never done this before, don't start now!

Best performance wins the job.

Joni turned to Owen and asked, "Have you ever skateboarded on an obstacle course?"

"Sure, zillions of times," Owen said with a grin. "It's called the streets of San Francisco."

"C'mon, I'm not joking."

"Neither am I," replied Owen, adjusting the slant of his rented blond stunt wig. "There isn't an obstacle course born that I can't handle."

"Um, excuse me, Owen," interrupted LapTrap, who was hovering above Joni's shoulder. "Obstacle courses aren't born, they're made—and they can be extremely dangerous."

"So?" said Owen.

"So maybe you should forget about this audition. We can see *The Doomsday Worm* when it comes out later in a nice, cool theater."

"What? And blow our chance to meet Perry Boston in person? No way!" Owen hunched down like a surfer catching an awesome wave. "Look out world!" he cried. "Owen Lam is hot."

"You're not the only one," moaned LapTrap. He gazed up anxiously at the blistering sun. Waves of heat rippled off his bright yellow casing. His brow dripped with sweat, and his internal cooling fan whirred at a maniac speed. "There are about twenty people ahead of us," he said. "By the time you try out, my chips will be fried."

"Just chill out, LapTrap," Santiago advised.

"How can I?" LapTrap protested. "I'm turning into a flying toaster."

"Here, I have just the thing for you," Santiago said. "It's one of my new inventions." From his back pocket he withdrew a metallic cigar-shaped object with a suction cup on one end. He stuck the rubber cup firmly onto LapTrap's lid, then pressed a button at the base of the tube. A paper-thin silver umbrella shot out of the top and sprang open to shade LapTrap from the sun. Seconds later, icicles formed along the edge of the umbrella.

"Hey, I really *am* chilling out," LapTrap exclaimed. "It's like I'm under an air-conditioner."

"You are," Santiago said with a smile. "It's my solar-powered frigibrella. It creates a swirling column of cold air underneath it."

"Excellent!" Owen said. "Say, Santiago, have you got another one for—"

Owen did not get to finish his sentence. A hush came over the crowd. It was eleven o'clock sharp. A short, balding man emerged from the studio and strode toward the front gates. He was wearing a loud Hawaiian shirt and a pair of electric-green Bermuda shorts that ended three inches above his dark purple cowboy boots. Tufts of sandy brown hair poked out like dust bunnies above his ears.

"All right, people—listen up!" the man said. "My name is Wilton Thumbling. I'm the director and producer of Boffo Pictures. In case you're wondering, I'm rich and famous, so I can dress any way I please. I'm also heartless and bossy. And if any of you have a problem with *that,* I suggest you leave right now." He stared up and down the line. No one moved. "Good," he said. "Then let the tryouts begin!"

Wilton Thumbling motioned to a guard to open the gates. Then he led the group into a gigantic building labeled Studio 43. There an assistant gave each contestant a call number. Owen's was twenty-two, which made him the next-to-last competitor.

The ClueFinders found seats on the edge of a vast set designed to look like New York City's Times Square. Behind them a narrow roadway looped around the set. On the roadway electric studio carts ferried actors, crew members, and props to and from key locations. Santiago took a digital video recorder out of his backpack. "I've got to film this," he said. "I'm sure we'll want to remember this whole scene for years to come."

Wilton Thumbling clapped his hands. "Okay, listen up, auditioners," he said. "As you may know, the young Perry Boston was quite a daredevil. He rode around on a jet skateboard he built himself. So before I give anybody a shot at the obstacle course, I want to see how well you can handle one of these…" He waved to another assistant, who whizzed up in an electric cart piled high with amazing-looking skateboards. Long and sleek, they all had gleaming wheels made of some ultra-strong, ultra-light metal. At the rear of each board was a stubby, cone-shaped jet engine.

"These babies are exact copies of the jetboard Perry Boston used when he captured Morris Nogudnik in Times Square," Wilton Thumbling continued. "My assistant, Attila"—he pointed to the man in the cart—"will escort you auditioners to the roadway that circles this set. I want each of you to make one lap on the jetboard. Attila will time you. The finishers with the three fastest times get to tackle the obstacle course."

Wilton Thumbling ordered the roadway cleared of all traffic. Then Attila led the contestants to the starting line, and the elimination round began. The ClueFinders watched in suspense as the contestants streaked by the viewing area one by one. LapTrap measured their times with radar pulses. Two hours later it was finally Owen's turn.

"Owen's got to beat two minutes and seventeen seconds to qualify," LapTrap announced nervously.

"I'm not worried," said Joni. "Owen can do it."

The starting gun went off. Owen surged forward and leaned into the first curve, disappearing behind the tall mock-ups of Times Square buildings. LapTrap picked him up again as he rounded the second turn and opened up the throttle in the straightaway. "Forty-nine seconds!" LapTrap exclaimed. "Best time so far."

"C'mon, Owen!" the ClueFinders screamed.

Owen poured on the heat, hugging the third turn like a comet whipping around the sun.

"One minute, twenty seconds," LapTrap said excitedly.

Owen took his final turn like a champ. He floored his jetboard and rocketed past the finish line. The spectators rose to their feet and roared their approval. Owen's final time was a stunning two minutes and three seconds.

Even Wilton Thumbling seemed impressed. "Monster performance, kid," he said. "Now let's see how you do on the obstacle course."

Wilton Thumbling dismissed all the auditioners except for Owen and the other two qualifiers, numbers seven and eleven. Then he climbed into his shooting chair, which was attached to the end of a long crane.

"Okay, places, people—places!" the director shouted. "Is the Nogudnik stunt double ready?"

"Ready, chief!" replied an otherwise ordinary-looking man bouncing up and down on a high-powered pogo stick.

Wilton Thumbling pushed a button and the arm of the crane lifted his chair high above the set. He peered down at the three finalists and said, "Okay, listen up. That guy on the pogo stick is a stunt man. He's playing the role of Morris Nogudnik, the world's greatest computer genius and pogo-stick rider. In this scene Nogudnik is being pursued by Perry Boston through Times Square. Your job, as Boston's stunt double, is to catch up with him. The yellow line on the floor marks the path you must follow. Any falls or wobbly performances and you're out. Got it?"

The three contestants nodded.

"Okay!" he bellowed. "Let's take number seven, eleven, then twenty-two. Ready on the set!"

Huge spotlights flashed on, revealing a fairy-tale vision of Times Square at dusk, complete with brilliant neon signs, stalled traffic, and street pushcarts. Above the set towered a working model of the mammoth Jumbotron videoscreen that ushers in the new year on TV every year.

"Cue the stunt guy!" Wilton Thumbling said. "Number seven—start your skateboard! And... ACTION!"

The set came alive. Taxis honked, pedestrians jaywalked, and brazen motorists tried to sneak through traffic lights. The stuntman playing Nogudnik bounded down "Broadway" in loopy arcs like a kangaroo on the moon. Skateboarder number seven tried to keep up, but he wiped out when a little old lady opened a taxi cab door into his path.

"Bye-bye," said Wilton Thumbling to number seven. "Have a nice rest of your life."

As the crew set up for the second test, Leslie turned to Joni and whispered, "I've always meant to ask you. How did Perry Boston apprehend Nogudnik?"

"It wasn't easy," Joni whispered back. "Perry Boston knew that Nogudnik had a weak spot. He was a word-game fanatic. He couldn't stand to see misspelled words and he could never leave a crossword puzzle unsolved. So Perry Boston used his wristwatch computer to tap into the Jumbotron and download a crossword puzzle onto the screen. When Nogudnik stopped to solve it, Perry Boston nabbed him."

"Ingenious," Leslie said admiringly.

Wilton Thumbling's voice boomed out again. "Ready on the set! Number eleven—start your jetboard! And... ACTION!"

Number eleven was an excellent jetboarder. He barely strayed six inches from the yellow line. When the little old lady opened her taxi door, he executed a flip that neatly avoided disaster. He was gaining on the stunt guy and had only a hundred yards to go.

"Cue the puzzle!" Wilton Thumbling yelled. A blinking crossword puzzle appeared on the Jumbotron under the bold heading "I DARE YOU TO SOLVE ME, NOGUDNIK!" The stunt guy playing Nogudnik halted under the Jumbotron and began bouncing up and down, trying to fill in the missing letters. That was when number seven failed to spot the pothole in the street. His front wheels lurched into it, his back wheels flew up, and number seven catapulted through the air, landing in a nail salon's awning.

"Can't anyone ride a jetboard like Perry Boston?" screamed Wilton Thumbling, pulling at the hair above his ears. "Twenty-two—you're next!" he snapped at Owen. "Don't disappoint me." Owen and the stunt guy took their starting positions.

"ACTION!" screamed Wilton Thumbling.

The stunt guy bounced and bounded but he couldn't shake Owen. The ClueFinder daredevil shot past the little old lady before she opened her door. All the jaywalkers, U-turners, and sudden blasts of steam from manholes didn't faze him one bit. He swerved around oil slicks, glided along guard rails, and somersaulted over sawhorses. Owen looked as if he'd been born on a jetboard. He was clearly the best boarder on the lot.

"Cue the puzzle!" Wilton Thumbling shouted in a voice trilling with joy. The crossword puzzle splashed across the Jumbotron. The stunt guy hit his mark and bounced in place. Owen skirted the killer pothole and closed in for the arrest.

FIZZ! POP! SPLOOONK! Suddenly the crossword puzzle vanished from the Jumbotron. Then the ghostly image of a toothless old woman dressed in a long robe appeared.

"Beware!" wailed the woman.

"Huh?" said the startled stuntman, who lost his grip on his pogo stick and began to fall. Owen kicked his jetboard into overdrive and managed to catch the man just before he hit the ground. Then Owen threw his jetboard into reverse. Slowly he brought it to a safe stop.

The ghostly woman still cackled on the screen. "Hear me, you wretches," she shrieked. "Leave this place. This movie is doooooooooomed!"

She shook a bony finger at the crew. "Beware!" she screeched again as her image gradually faded. Then—*BOOM* —after a quick explosion, sparks showered down on everyone from the computer control room overhead.

Solve the crossword puzzle for the ClueFinders.

1 A movie _ _ _ _

2 ClueFinders' home town (initials)_ _

3 Boffo director's hairstyle_ _ _ _ _

4 Wilton_ _ _ _ _ _ _ _ _

5 The _ _ _ _ Finders

6 Perry Boston's "stunt_ _ _ _ _ _"

7 Joni _ _ _ _ _ _

SABOTAGE!

Joni shot out of her chair. "Follow me, guys!" she called. Leslie and Santiago instinctively fell in behind her.

"Wait!" cried LapTrap. "You're going the wrong way. The fire exit is in the opposite direction."

A slender metal ladder was all that connected the ground level of the set to a steel bridge that spanned the width of the building. On top of the bridge sat a glass-enclosed room with a wide, commanding view of the entire set. Inside, a man was struggling to bring his malfunctioning computers under control.

Joni scampered up the ladder. She reached the room before anyone else.

"Here, catch this!" she said, grabbing an electrical fire extinguisher from the wall and tossing it to the computer operator.

"Just what I need!" shouted the man, who aimed a blast of smothering foam onto the short-circuiting wires.

Santiago and Leslie burst through the door.

"What can we do?" cried Santiago.

Joni's eyes darted around the room. "Find the circuit breakers and cut the power to this booth. Leslie—grab the documents and disks."

Joni picked up a small rug and began beating out a paper fire that had flared up on the computer operator's desk. Soon more help arrived and all the smoldering fires had been put out. Then the weary firefighters straggled down to the street level of the Times Square set.

Wilton Thumbling lowered his shooting chair and hopped out. "I don't know who you and your friends are," he said to Joni. "But your quick thinking saved our computer equipment."

"Don't mention it," Joni said. "We're the ClueFinders. Number twenty-two is a member of our group. We solve mysteries."

Wilton Thumbling raised his eyebrows. "Then I owe you ClueFinders double thanks. Your buddy saved my stunt man." Wilton Thumbling's eyes glistened. "If I were a nicer guy, I would probably do something nice for you. But I'm not, so I won't."

Joni frowned. "Actually, there is something you can do for us and it won't cost you anything."

"Eh, what's that?"

"You could tell us whether Owen—I mean, number twenty-two—got the job."

Wilton Thumbling laughed. "Kid," he said, "I like your style. Your friend is a monster boarder. The job's his if he wants it."

The ClueFinders whooped for joy.

"But let's get one thing straight," Wilton Thumbling continued. "That's not me being nice. That's me being *smart*."

Joni looked around. Owen, still at the far end of the set, was tending to the badly shaken stuntman. Joni sent Santiago to tell Owen the good news.

"W.T.?" interrupted the computer control operator.

"What is it, Binckley?" Wilton Thumbling asked.

"If these kids are mystery-solvers, maybe we can use them to investigate the *thing* on the Jumbotron. And who sabotaged the control panel."

"*Sabotage*?" Joni said, her blue eyes widening. "How can you be so sure, Mr. Binckley?"

The computer operator's expression grew grave. "I program all effects on this set, including what appears on the Jumbotron. Nobody has access to the computers but me. And I can tell you right now that I never programmed any banshee to appear."

"*Banshee?*" replied Joni. "What's that?"

Leslie, who knew practically everything, volunteered an explanation. "A banshee is a female spirit from Irish folklore. It has a blood-curdling wail, which is believed to foretell an imminent calamity."

"I see," Joni said. Then she turned back to Binckley. "Are you saying you believe the fire had something to do with that... that banshee?"

"All I know is that my computers lost power the instant that creature appeared on the Jumbotron. And when I tried to regain control, the circuits started blowing everywhere."

"So the Jumbotron should have gone dark?" interjected Santiago, who had returned with an insanely happy Owen.

"Right," Binckley said. "It was getting no electricity."

"Yet it lit up with that banshee," Santiago said. "How do you explain that?"

Binckley shrugged. "I can't. That's why I think you guys can help. We can't call in the police—the studio wouldn't like the bad publicity. But you could do some quiet sleuthing behind the scenes."

"Excellent idea, Binckley," said Wilton

Thumbling. Then he turned to Joni and gave her a searching look. "Can you promise me that you and your friends will handle this assignment *discreetly*?"

"Absolutely," replied Joni. "But you've got to let us go anywhere and question anyone we'd like."

"It's a deal," Wilton Thumbling said, pumping Joni's hand. Then he reached into his pocket and gave Joni a key dotted with sparkling microchips. "This will get you into all Boffo buildings and rooms," he said. "Use it wisely."

Wilton Thumbling faced the rest of the crew. "Okay, listen up, everyone!" he said. "We've got our stunt double and we've also got a big mess to clean up. Everyone take the rest of today off, except the maintenance crew. See you early tomorrow morning." With that, he wheeled around on his boot heels and strutted toward the rear of the set.

Before the ClueFinders left the building, Attila gave Owen some papers to sign and handed him his official BOFFO PICTURES' PERPETUAL PIZZA CARD. "Can I use it today?" Owen asked.

"Certainly," replied Attila. "The best place to eat is the Pizzaroma. Simply follow the path across the studio grounds. It's about a block away from the front gates. You can't miss it."

◧▧◩

The path back to the entrance also proved to be the scenic route. It wound through dozens of studios, outdoor sets, and production facilities. In each studio a different movie was being filmed. Actors and extras in colorful makeup and fancy costumes spilled over into the alleyways or sat on cement benches awaiting their scenes. In less than thirty minutes, the ClueFinders passed actors dressed as giant crabs, ancient Roman gladiators, punk rockers, Santa's elves, and English chimney sweeps.

"This is way fun," Joni said. "This place is like a dream factory."

As they approached the gate, a man in a space alien costume darted in front of them. He had three green eyes, large orange gills on both sides of his neck, a glowing antenna that bobbed from his forehead, and hairy, cup-shaped ears.

"You're the ClueFinders, aren't you?" he asked in a wheezing voice.

"Er—yes, how did you know?" Joni said.

"I've read about your cases. One day you may be as famous as Perry Boston."

"Nice of you to say," Joni said. "But he's a crime-fighter. We solve mysteries."

"You know, I would have recognized you five
anywhere," the alien babbled on. "Watch, I'll prove
it."

"No need," Joni replied politely. "I believe you."

The alien ignored her. He pointed out the
ClueFinders one by one. "You're Joni, the fearless
leader. You're Santiago, the brainy inventor. You're
Leslie, the information superstar. You're Owen, the
daredevil sportsdude. And you're LapTrap, the
flying supercomputer." The alien smiled. "You see,"
he said. "I know all about you."

"Look, we're all very flattered," Joni said. "But
we really have to get going."

"No, wait!" he said, blocking her path. "Purely
out of curiosity, what brings you here to Boffo? Is it
business or pleasure?"

"Would you please let us by?" Joni asked curtly.
When the alien refused to budge, Joni faked right,
lurched left, and swung around him. As the alien
tried to recover, Leslie, Santiago, and LapTrap ran
around him on the other side.

"Ugh! That guy gave me the creeps," Joni said
once they were out of earshot.

"Me, too," agreed Santiago.

"I seriously doubt he was a ClueFinders fan," Leslie added.

"You can say that again," Joni said.

"Owen seems to be getting along with him fine, however," LapTrap volunteered.

Santiago stopped short. "Owen? Didn't he follow us?"

"No, he's still talking with that alien gentleman," remarked LapTrap.

"He's doing *WHAT*?" exclaimed Joni. The ClueFinders spun around. There was Owen, laughing and chatting away with the nosy stranger, who was frantically jotting notes on a yellow pad.

"I've got a bad feeling about this," Santiago said.

"Me, too," Joni agreed. She broke into a run. "C'mon, guys! I've got a few personal questions of my own for Mr. Alien."

At the sound of approaching footsteps, the alien jerked his head up, saw the ClueFinders, and began backing away.

"Owen, stop that guy!" yelled Santiago. "We want to question him."

"Hey, wait a minute, dude," Owen shouted at the alien now lumbering across the grass. The alien jumped a chain-link fence and dashed toward a long brick building. Owen vaulted the fence after him. Although the alien had a lead, he was no match for the speedy Owen. In desperation, the alien veered into a blind alley.

"You're trapped, dude!" Owen cried.

"That's what you think!" Mr. Alien called back, whereupon he charged full tilt into—and *RIGHT THROUGH!!*—a solid brick wall.

The ClueFinders stopped and gaped at the spot where the man in the alien outfit had made his astonishing exit.

"Owen, what did you tell that guy?" said Santiago, gasping for breath.

"He wanted to know about my audition and the banshee and how Wilton Thumbling reacted."

"But what did you *tell* him?" Joni demanded.

Owen gulped. "Sort of everything."

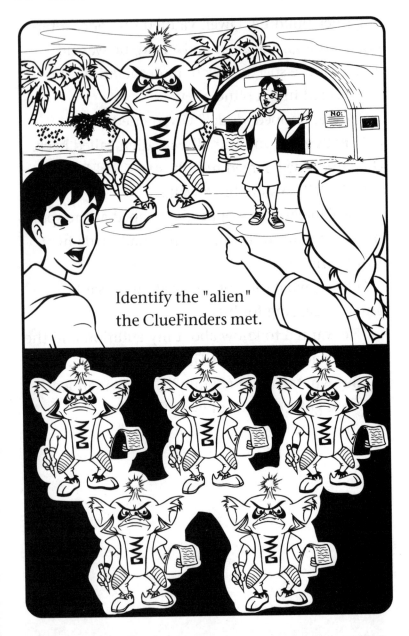

Identify the "alien" the ClueFinders met.

OUT OF THE SHADOWS

At the next day's shoot, the actors and crew had to make up for lost time because of the banshee incident. While Owen met with the stunt coach to discuss his upcoming routines, the ClueFinders gathered secretly in an upstairs audio recording room. Joni, Santiago, and Leslie sat in a semicircle facing LapTrap's brilliant liquid crystal screen.

Joni pitched forward in her seat, sending her long red braids tumbling over her shoulders. "Okay, guys, what do we know so far?"

Leslie pursed her lips. "Well, we know that someone is out to disrupt Wilton Thumbling's movie, but we don't know who or why."

"And we know that the person who created the banshee has some pretty awesome technical skills," Santiago added.

"How do we know that?" questioned Joni.

"Simple," Santiago said. "The culprit was able to hijack Mr. Binckley's computers and run an image of the banshee on the Jumbotron."

"Didn't Mr. Binckley say his computers lost

power?" Leslie asked. How could a banshee appear on a powerless Jumbotron?"

"Good question," Santiago replied, scratching his head. "That's been bugging me, too."

"Do you think Binckley's lying?" Joni asked.

"It's not impossible," Santiago said.

"While we're on the subject of impossibilities," Leslie said, "does anybody have any theories about our friendly alien?"

Santiago raised his hand. "My best guess is that he was some sort of illusion—maybe a hologram."

"What's that?" asked Joni.

"A hologram is a three-dimensional image created on a two-dimensional surface or in free space by means of light interference," Leslie explained.

"Sounds complicated," Joni said.

"It is," Santiago said. "And that's the one flaw with my hunch. No one has ever created a hologram like Mr. Alien that can walk and talk and trick you into believing it's alive."

"I see," Joni said.

"Our problem gets worse," Santiago added. "I checked with Wilton Thumbling's office this morning. No pictures about aliens are being filmed at Boffo. So we've got absolutely zero leads."

Leslie sighed. "It's all so diabolically frustrating," she said. "I wish we could replay exactly what happened when the banshee appeared. That might give us some clues."

Santiago sat up abruptly. "Wait a minute!" he exclaimed. "We *can* replay what happened. I filmed the whole thing. I can download the tape onto LapTrap's hard drive and we can examine it frame by frame."

A few minutes later the video was ready for viewing. "I've asked LapTrap to draw a grid on each frame," Santiago said. "That way we can zoom in on any square in the picture."

The ClueFinders huddled around LapTrap's screen. "Play it from the point where the crossword puzzle vanishes," Joni instructed LapTrap.

As the action unfolded, Joni's jaw dropped open. "Stop, LapTrap!" she cried. "Go back a few frames."

LapTrap reversed the sequence; then he played it again.

"Incredible!" Joni exclaimed.

"What do you see?" asked Leslie.

"Bring up the first shot of the banshee, LapTrap," Joni said. "Then enlarge row K."

LapTrap zoomed in on a narrow strip of the grid. It showed a gray-green area that wrapped around the bottom edge of the Jumbotron. "Do you see it now?" Joni asked.

"All I see is the banshee's shadow," Leslie replied.

"Correct," Joni said. "But see where it falls?"

"Outside the Jumbotron."

"Exactly."

"I still don't get it," Leslie said.

"Look, there's no way a two-dimensional image can cast a real shadow."

"Of course!" exclaimed Santiago. "The banshee was never actually *on* the Jumbotron. She was *in front* of it. That's why her shadow spilled over."

"Right," said Joni. "And that answers the question of how a powerless Jumbotron could produce electronic images. It *didn't*. It just looked like it did from below."

"Then Mr. Binckley was probably telling us the truth," Leslie said.

"Perhaps," Joni said. "But I think Santiago got it right. Whoever is behind all of this must be some kind of scientific genius—who takes pleasure in making fools of us."

The ClueFinders returned to the set to find Wilton Thumbling directing Jason Torch, the blond superstar, in an escape scene from *The Doomsday Worm*. A room resembling a dungeon had been built in a far corner of Studio 43. The young actor playing the role of Perry Boston was sitting in a barber's chair with a gray plastic helmet over his head. Thick ropes bound him fast to the chair. A tiny TV aerial poked out of the top of the helmet.

"No! I need more feeling, Jason!" Wilton Thumbling was shouting. "Let's take it again."

"But I can't see or breathe in this thing, W.T.," Jason Torch complained.

"Excellent!" Wilton Thumbling said. "You're supposed to be suffering in this scene. Remember, you've been captured by Morris Nogudnik, and for the past three days, he's been beaming nonstop zit-cream commercials directly into your brain through your helmet. Your mind is turning to mush."

"My mind *is* turning to mush, W.T.," Jason Torch replied in a muffled voice.

"That's the spirit!" Wilton Thumbling said, rapping Jason Torch on the helmet and hopping into his shooting chair. "Okay, Jason, just as you're about to snap, you remember that Morris Nogudnik shuts his computers down by singing 'London Bridge Is Falling Down.' You wonder if you can stop the brain-drainer by doing the same."

"Got it, W.T."

"Okay, people, let's take it from the top."

Santiago gave Joni a nudge. "This is *s-o-o-o* exciting!"

"Cue the glockenspiel music! And... ACTION!"

Jason Torch began squirming and grunting in his chair. From inside his helmet came a desperate, gurgling sound:

Longin Glitch is fawding down,
Fawding gown, fawting gown,
London Brizz is galling frown, my —

Suddenly Jason stopped gurgling the nursery rhyme and began singing an entirely different song in a high-pitched woman's voice:

I've warned you once.
I've come anew.
To curse this film
And all its crew.

"CUT!!" groaned Wilton Thumbling. He stormed over to the barber's chair and yanked off Jason Torch's helmet. "What are you doing?" he asked. "Those lines aren't in the script."

Jason Torch breathed heavily. "This helmet... it really took over... felt waves in my brain... had to say those words ... couldn't help myself..."

With a big whoosh of air, the bad news banshee swooped down from the rafters. "This is only a taste of what I can do," she screeched. "I can control the minds of your actors. End this film while you can!" Then, with a loud cackle, she dove into a half-empty soda bottle and *POOFED!* out of sight.

The movie crew stood frozen in fear. The ClueFinders rushed to inspect the bottle. There was nothing in it but orange soda.

Practically unnoticed, a chunky, blond-haired figure in a baseball jacket stepped out of the shadows. He had twinkly blue eyes and a scruffy blond beard. His right arm was fixed in a sling inside his jacket.

"Perhaps I can be of assistance," he said. "My name is Perry Boston."

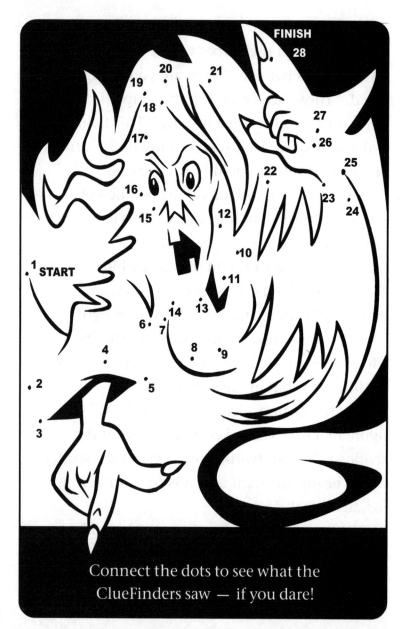

Connect the dots to see what the
ClueFinders saw — if you dare!

CHAPTER 5

DISCOVERED!

"Mr. Boston!" Joni said. "Great to meet you." She extended her hand.

"Sorry, can't shake," Perry Boston said, pointing to his injured arm. "Bad accident in my pencil-eraser factory. Broke it in two places. Can't even sign my name."

Joni gazed at the immobilized arm. "How awful," she said.

Perry Boston sighed. "What can you do? A few years of retirement and you're slipping on pencil erasers left and right. With whom do I have the pleasure of speaking?"

"We're the ClueFinders, a detective team from San Francisco," Joni said. "I'm Joni, and these are three of my teammates—Santiago, Leslie, and LapTrap."

"Ah, yes," Perry Boston said with a broad grin. "Wilton Thumbling told me to look out for a group of sharp-eyed young investigators."

"Only doing our job," Joni said. She quickly brought the subject back to the banshee. "You said you could help us, Mr. Boston. Do you know anything about this matter?"

Perry Boston glanced around suspiciously. "Lots," he whispered. "Where can we talk?"

Joni thought for a minute. "We ate at a nice restaurant yesterday," she suggested. "It's called The Pizzaroma. We're meeting our other teammate, Owen, there. He's playing your stunt double in the movie. Want to join us?"

"Absolutely," Perry Boston replied. "But if you don't mind, I'll just watch you youngsters eat."

The Pizzaroma was a popular lunchtime hangout for Boffo Pictures employees. Housed in a circular flat-roofed building shaped like a pepperoni pizza, it had a puffy, golden-colored "crust" exterior made of cement, with a missing wedge for its entrance. Inside the Pizzaroma, the walls were decorated with posters of the Coliseum and other classic Roman ruins. Customers sat at round speckled tables resembling pepperoni slices. It was definitely the place to be—and be seen—during lunchtime.

After the ClueFinders ordered, Santiago plugged LapTrap's recharger into a nearby wall outlet.

"Mmmmmmm..." said the hungry laptop, "parmesan-flavored electrons!"

By the time the pizzas came, the lunch crowd had thinned out, the noise had settled down to a manageable roar, and Perry Boston had dropped a bombshell of a revelation.

"You mean, you think *Wilton Thumbling* is behind all this?" Joni said with surprise.

"Correct," Perry Boston said.

Joni took the idea in slowly. "It doesn't make any sense. Why would Wilton Thumbling want to destroy his own picture?"

"Joni's right," said Santiago. "And why would he ask us to investigate if he thought it might lead us to expose him?"

LapTrap's charger light turned green. Santiago unplugged his cables and let him float contentedly above the table.

"I'll answer you in two words," Perry Boston said. "*Money* and *vanity*."

"I'm not sure I follow," Joni said.

"It's simple," Perry Boston went on. "Thumbling's movie is way over budget. If it fails now, he stands to collect a hefty amount in insurance. I saw the insurance contracts on his desk when I signed my consulting deal."

"What about Santiago's point?" Leslie asked.

"I was getting to that," Perry Boston said. "Wilton Thumbling is not a humble man. He feels he's too smart to get caught. What better way to divert attention from himself than to launch his own very 'private' investigation? My dears, he's using you. Think about it. He had the motive, the opportunity—and the equipment."

Santiago's ears perked up. "What kind of equipment?"

Perry Boston leaned over the table and lowered his voice. "I suggest you check out room 310-W in Studio 43. That's where Thumbling conducts weekend tests of a revolutionary new motion picture system. If it works, it will change the industry forever. It's a 3-D hologram projector."

The ClueFinders gasped. This was exactly the kind of device Santiago had been talking about.

"I'm bummed," Owen said, slumping down in his seat. "My director-dude is a crook! I gotta have more pizza to steady my nerves."

"Knowing Owen's appetite, I'm afraid this could take another hour, Mr. Boston," Leslie said.

"I see," said Perry Boston, smiling. Time for me

to go. I have to make an important call. Urgent pencil-eraser business. I'm sure you understand."

The ClueFinders nodded.

"I'll let you know if I learn anything new," he said in parting.

The ClueFinders sat in silence, contemplating the information Perry Boston had shared.

Santiago finally spoke. "You know, I had a funny feeling about Wilton Thumbling from the start."

Joni tapped her fork distractedly on the tabletop. "We've got to gather more evidence."

"Don't you trust Perry Boston?" Santiago asked.

"Even Perry Boston wouldn't take Perry Boston's word for it," replied Joni. "He'd demand proof."

"How are we going to get it?" Santiago asked.

"The usual way—dig for it," Joni said. She placed a hand on Leslie's shoulder. "Leslie, would you check out the newspapers and movie magazines in the library? See if you can verify that *The Doomsday Worm* is way over budget."

"Roger!" Leslie replied.

Next Joni turned to Santiago. She handed him Wilton Thumbling's master key. "Find out if there really is a banshee projector in room 310-W. Since Wilton Thumbling tests the machine on weekends, you'd better wait until Monday to go in."

"I'm all over that," Santiago replied.

"Hey, what about me?" asked Owen.

"Your beat is the set," Joni instructed. "Watch Wilton Thumbling like a hawk. See if he does anything suspicious."

"Ahem!" LapTrap said, clearing his throat loudly. "Didn't you forget someone? Someone very important!"

Just then, a deeply tanned woman with her hair tied back tightly passed the ClueFinders' table. She wore a black satin jump suit and a multi-ringed necklace of gold seahorses. On a thin, oil-stained sheet of paper she held a limp slice of pizza. At the sound of LapTrap's voice she stopped cold, whirled around, and cried out, "Say that again!"

LapTrap rotated in mid-air to face the woman. "Excuse me, are you talking to me?"

"Marvelous, dar-ling! Sim-ply marvelous," the woman said. She dropped her slice with a SPLAT! onto Owen's plate.

"Gee, thanks!" Owen said, digging in.

The woman stared raptly into LapTrap's big round eyes. "Say this," she ordered. "*The sit-u-ation's grim, Cap-tain Boom-bah. It looks like the e-vil mon-key king has jammed our quark fib-ril-la-tors!"*

"Um, *The sit-u-ation's grim, Cap-tain Boom-bah. It looks like the e-vil mon-key king has jammed our quark fib-ril-la-tors!"*

"Perfect! Ut-ter-ly perfect!" she said, clapping.

"It is?" said LapTrap.

"Yesss." The woman reached into her pocketbook, grabbed a business card, and stuck it into LapTrap's disk drive.

"Have you ever been in pictures, dar-ling?"

"Me? N-n-no," stammered LapTrap.

"You should. You have such expressive eye-brows, such sweep-ing planes, such fine-ly chiseled corners, such a dominating lid."

"You really think so?" LapTrap said, trying to catch a reflection of himself in a nearby window.

"I know so, treasure," the woman said. "I am Lulu Randango, the famous sci-fi direc-tor. I have discovered the great-est robot and droid actors of all time. I take dull, gray pieces of hard-ware and turn them into shin-ing stars."

"I'm not gray," LapTrap said.

"Gray-shmay. It makes no difference."

LapTrap's eyes widened into saucers. "You mean, you want to make me—LapTrap—a movie star?"

"Yes, my lit-tle silicon pump-kin. Come see me on Wednesday at Boffo Pic-tures in Studio 9. I will give you a screen test for my next picture. With that voice, those rectangles, those eye-brows, you are a nat-u-ral!" She paused. "By the way, do you have an e-mail ad-dress?"

LapTrap gave it to her.

"Good," she said. "I will e-mail you your lines." Then she kissed LapTrap on his lid, leaving a splotchy red lipstick print on his shiny yellow coat. "Good-bye for now," Lulu Randango said in a voice thick with drama. "I must flee and cre-ate!"

Lulu Randango *click-clacked* out of Pizzaroma's entrance on her stiletto high heels.

Joni followed Lulu with her eyes. "Oh, brother," she muttered, letting her head sink into her hands. "Isn't anyone in Hollywood even a little bit sane?"

LapTrap floated airily upwards and sighed dreamily. "Imagine, guys, I'm going to be in motion pictures."

PIZZA

Select Your Toppings

anchovies

asparagus

banana

bleu cheese

broccoli

carrots

cheddar cheese

chicken

cucumber

garlic

green beans

herring

huckleberries

meatballs

mint

mushrooms

olives

onion

peanuts

pepperoni

raisins

red pepper

rutabaga

sausage

squash

strawberries

tofu

tuna

turnips

Look at the toppings and find:

Three that are fish. Four with four syllables.
Two that are verbs. Four that start with vowels.
One that's a fungus.

SANTIAGO MAKES A FRIM-FRAM

An overcast morning had turned the sky into a dull gray inverted bowl. Joni parted the curtains in the common room of the ClueFinders' hotel suite and gazed pensively at the drizzling rain. She'd been rereading Perry Boston's autobiography, *Extreme Measures: The Life of a Daredevil Crime Fighter,* in hopes of gaining new insights into how to approach the banshee case. But halfway through the book she'd put it down.

Both the weather and the ClueFinders' investigation were in a holding pattern. Leslie was off doing research at the library. In the adjoining boys' suite, Owen was helping LapTrap memorize lines for his upcoming screen test.

Joni was growing tired of hearing LapTrap intone about *Cap-tain Boom-bah* and the *e-vil monkey king.*

Santiago was with Joni, but only in the narrowest of senses. Physically, he was sitting on the nearby couch, tinkering with what looked like a TV remote control. Mentally, he was lost in his own world of science and technology.

With a sigh, Joni closed the curtains and plunked herself down beside him, drawing her knees up to her chest. "What's that?" she asked.

Santiago snapped the top of the remote shut. "If it works as it's supposed to," he said, "it will block all photonic standing-wave interference patterns within a five-hundred-yard radius."

Joni nodded knowingly. "Oh, now I get it." She pointed to a large blue button. "So you push this thing and the frim-fram exuviates a hoohah, resulting in a zoogalosis of the blahdeeblah."

"Huh? What are you babbling about?" Santiago laughed.

"*Me*? No, *you*!" Joni retorted. "Tell me what you're making—in plain English."

"Okay, okay." Santiago smiled and handed Joni the keypad. "Put simply, this instrument is designed to block the light waves that produce holograms. It should make them disappear so that they can't scare anybody."

Joni scrutinized the device's careful workmanship. "You're amazing, Santiago. What would the ClueFinders do without you?"

"I'll accept your compliments if and when it

actually works," Santiago said modestly.

The rain fell for hours. When Leslie returned from the library, Joni gathered the ClueFinders for a meeting. She asked Santiago to report on his new invention. Then she turned the floor over to Leslie.

Leslie flipped through some notes on a lined pad. "Perry Boston was right," she began. "*The Doomsday Worm* is way over budget. And—get this!—I found an old clipping that said Boffo Pictures was working on a secret new movie technology. Wilton Thumbling told a reporter that he would demonstrate it soon and that he believed it would make Boffo billions."

"Interesting," Joni observed. "A banshee scare could help Thumbling in one of two ways. If it halts the movie, he collects the insurance. If it doesn't, he can claim the banshee was a publicity stunt to promote his invention."

"So he wins if he wins and he wins if he loses," Santiago said.

"Exactly," said Leslie.

"It all seems to fit neatly," Joni observed, "but if Thumbling's operating the hologram projector, how could he and the banshee be in the same place at the same time?"

"That's easy," said Santiago. "He probably has someone else operating the machine—or maybe it works on a timer or by remote control."

"Maybe," Joni said. "But I still think there's more to this case than meets the eye. Wilton Thumbling may be brilliant at making movies, but you can be sure he's no scientific genius."

◙◙

Upon arriving at Boffo Pictures on Monday morning, the ClueFinders split up to pursue their different assignments. Santiago headed for room 310-W. LapTrap flew weary circles around the backlot in case the banshee or alien made another appearance. Joni and Leslie covered the action on the set. Owen monitored the actors and crew backstage.

On the set Jason Torch was rehearsing a scene with Vince DeGrotto, the actor cast as Morris Nogudnik. Joni and Leslie and Perry Boston sat on a large black trunk watching the run-through.

"He wouldn't have been my first pick for the part," Perry Boston whispered to Joni.

"Who?" Joni whispered back.

"Vince DeGrotto. He's too ordinary to play

Morris Nogudnik. Morris had more class."

"Really?" Joni remarked. "I didn't get that impression from your book."

"Editors—they twisted my words. Sells more books."

"No kidding. Who would have thought?"

Vince DeGrotto was a middle-aged actor with a sunken face and deep, sad eyes ringed with dark shadows. His short, wiry hair, which stood out straight as porcupine quills, gave him the startling appearance of a nerd who'd accidentally poked his finger into an electric outlet. For years he'd delighted viewers as the nearsighted and clumsy dentist, "Mr. Ugly," on the hit sitcom *The Losers*. *The Doomsday Worm* was his first shot at a starring role in a major motion picture.

"Actually, I don't think he's ordinary-looking at all," Leslie said. "He's got expressive eyes and a highly evocative face."

Perry Boston grew irritated. "Vince DeGrotto is nothing but a second-rate comedian. He's not worthy of the role of my greatest enemy."

"C'mon, Mr. Boston, lighten up," Joni chided. "Vince DeGrotto really can act, you know. *The Losers* won a lot of awards."

FWEEEET-TWEEEET!!!

Joni's videophone chirped inside her backpack.

FWEEEET-TWEEEET!!!

Wilton Thumbling exploded in anger. "WILL WHOEVER'S PHONE WENT OFF *PUH-LEASE* TAKE HIS CONVERSATION ELSEWHERE!"

Joni's face reddened. She hastily retrieved her videophone and clicked it on. Santiago's face popped up on the TV screen.

"Hold on, Santiago," Joni whispered. "I can't talk here." Leaving Perry Boston by himself, Joni and Leslie scurried over to an empty costume room and plunked themselves down on a bench.

"Okay, we're alone now," Joni said with relief. "Where are you?"

"I'm in 310-W," Santiago said.

"*And?*"

"I found a 3-D hologram machine."

"Great! You're sure that's what it is?"

"Positive. I even got it to work a little. But here's the weird part. This machine only produces black and white holograms—and they're not interactive."

"Meaning...?"

"There's no way this machine could produce a 3-D hologram as realistic as Mr. Alien."

"You're sure?"

"Totally."

"Could Wilton Thumbling have a more advanced machine hidden elsewhere?"

"Unh-uh," Santiago said. "He's got a whole library of holographic movies here. But they all have recent dates and they're all animations. It looks like Wilton Thumbling's big invention is a 3-D holographic cartoon machine."

Joni's face fell. "Okay, good work, Santiago. Hurry down and join us on the set."

Joni flicked off the videophone and muttered to Leslie, who had overheard everything, "Looks like we're back to square one again."

Room 310-W was on the sixth floor of Studio 43's business wing. As Santiago ambled down the corridor, he noticed Wilton Thumbling's office door hanging open. A flash of orange caught his eye.

"Hello?" he said, poking his head inside.

"Well, Santiago," a familiar voice answered. "We meet again."

The alien was standing behind Wilton Thumbling's desk.

"What are you doing here?" Santiago asked.

"Same as you—snooping." The alien grinned. "Are you scared?"

"You don't scare me," Santiago replied. "You're nothing but a hologram."

"Smart boy. You've guessed my secret," Mr. Alien said. "But you won't thwart my plans."

"You're not going to get away this time," Santiago said.

The alien laughed scornfully. His hideous gills swelled like bullfrog cheeks. "What are you going to do? Put a brick wall in my path?"

"No, I've got something better—a photonic blocker," Santiago replied calmly. He withdrew the device from his pocket.

The alien turned pale around the gills, as if he understood full well what Santiago's invention could do. "You'll have to catch me first!" he said, leaping through the office wall.

Santiago dashed into the corridor. The alien streaked toward the elevator doors. Santiago pointed the blocker at the fleeing hologram and set its power level at MILD. "You mind holding those doors for me?" he asked. "I'm going your way." He pushed the button marked ENTER.

A corkscrew of pink light enveloped the alien. His suit erupted in a storm of sparks. "*AAARRRGH!!!*" he cried as he dove at the steel elevator doors... and rebounded into the hall.

"Hey, that's not supposed to happen!" he howled.

"My blocker neutralizes your ability to pass through solid objects," Santiago explained.

"You're not playing fair!" the alien said. Then he turned and made for the stairway.

Santiago took off in hot pursuit. He chased the alien down five flights of stairs and out into the bright sunlight of the backlot. He spotted the alien slipping into the Broadcast Center, where *Blankety-Blank!*, Boffo's popular TV quiz program, was being videotaped before a live audience.

Santiago followed the alien into the building and through a maze of backstage passageways that ended at a huge velvet curtain. The quiz program had started on the other side. Through the curtain Santiago could hear the host of *Blankety-Blank!* addressing the contestants:

"All right, folks, I'm sure you know how the game's played. Today's puzzle board contains six words with only the vowels filled in. You have two minutes to figure out what the words are. The clues are in your envelopes. Ready? Set. Go!"

Organ music began playing softly in the background. Suddenly the music stopped. People in the audience screamed. Santiago knew that could mean only one thing—the alien was out there somewhere! Santiago pulled back the curtain and stepped onto the *Blankety-Blank!* stage. He saw the announcer cringing in fear under the puzzle board. The audience was standing, pointing at the alien, who was terrorizing one of the contestants. "Hurry up! Solve the puzzle!" the sinister hologram shouted. "I can't do it myself. Do you think I can hold a pencil? No, that's not a 'D', it's an 'R'."

"Omigosh!" Santiago exclaimed. "It's all clear now. I know who created the banshee and Mr. Alien. How could we be so blind?" He took out his photonic blocker and switched the power to MAX STRENGTH. "Bye-bye, Mr. Alien," he said. "You won't bother anyone again." Then he pressed ENTER.

This time the blast of pink light zapped the alien hard. "Rats!" he cried. The 3-D hologram twisted and warped out of shape like a stretched balloon. Then it shriveled into pink nothingness like a mouthful of cotton candy.

Use clues from the story to solve the
Blankety-Blank! puzzle.

1. Another word for a film
2. A person who stars in a movie
3. The words an actor must learn
4. Where a film is shown
5. The machine used to shoot a movie
6. Stuff actors wear on their faces

"DOUBLE, DOUBLE, TOIL AND TROUBLE"

Leslie searched the Internet on LapTrap that evening and confirmed Santiago's new theory about the case. "Here's the lead story from last month's *Prisoners' Jailbreak Times,*" she said, laying it on the coffee table in the common room for all to see. The article read:

Nogudnik Pulls Vanishing Act of Century

You can't keep a no-good man down. That's what prison officials at the Federal Prison for Misguided Geniuses (FPMG) are saying today in the wake of the baffling disappearance of FPMG inmate Morris Nogudnik. Nobody knows exactly how or when Mr. Nogudnik made his daring escape, because he left behind a walking, talking hologram of himself that fooled prison officials into believing he was safely behind bars. Corrections Officer R. Stinky Hubbaboo discovered the trick when he accidentally put his arm through the hologram's.

"He pulled a fast one on us," commented Warden Irving W. Mulegullet III.

Mr. Nogudnik, best known for his attempt to "eat the Internet" with a so-called Doomsday Worm, had lately become discontented with jail and had been overheard saying something about taking revenge on his arch-enemy Perry Boston, and on a Hollywood movie director who was also working on a hologram invention.

"So our man is Morris Nogudnik, up to his old tricks again," Owen said, whistling.

"Exactly," Santiago said. "I knew it the minute Mr. Alien stopped to solve the *Blankety-Blank!* puzzle. He was behaving just like Morris Nogudnik."

"But why didn't Mr. Alien pick up a pencil, solve the puzzle, and get out of there?" Owen asked.

"Because a hologram *looks* real," Santiago explained, "but it can't do real things, like hold a pencil."

Owen still looked confused. "But what about the computer-room fire and the helmet that made Jason Torch talk like the banshee? They were real."

"Sure," Santiago said. "But don't forget Morris Nogudnik can hack into any computer with ease. And he knows how to control people's minds."

"I agree," Joni said. "Nobody but Nogudnik could pull all of this off. The problem is that he could create millions of holograms of himself. We could wind up chasing mirages for years."

"I'm not so sure," Santiago said. "It takes an awful lot of computer power to make an interactive hologram. Plus, we've never actually seen more than one hologram at a time."

"—or anywhere but at Boffo Pictures," Leslie observed. "If Nogudnik is operating holograms by remote control, I bet he's not far away."

Santiago slapped his forehead. *"Duh!* You're brilliant, Leslie."

"I am?"

Santiago nodded. "Look, my photonic blocker only works if a hologram is within fifteen hundred feet of Nogudnik's transmitter."

"So?"

"So it worked once in Studio 43 and once in the Broadcast Center." He opened a notebook and drew two overlapping circles on a piece of paper. He labeled the center of one circle "Studio 43" and the center of the other "Broadcast Center."

"Of course!" Leslie said. "It's basic geometry. Morris Nogudnik's machine has to be somewhere within the overlapping area."

"Exactly," Santiago said. He motioned to

LapTrap. "Come here, little buddy. I need you."

A few minutes later the ClueFinders were staring at a detailed map of the Boffo Pictures backlot, on which LapTrap had drawn scaled versions of Santiago's circles. The overlapping area was highlighted in yellow.

Joni examined the map closely. "I count six possible buildings in the yellow zone."

"Before we do anything," Leslie interjected, "don't you think we should call Perry Boston?"

Joni scrunched up her nose. "You know," she said, "I'm not sure I trust him anymore."

The other ClueFinders looked shocked.

"Why?" Santiago asked.

Joni found Perry Boston's autobiography on the table, and showed everyone a picture of the crime fighter. "What do you see?" she said.

"He's signing autographs," said Owen.

"With which hand?"

"His left. What's the big deal?"

Joni nodded and went on, "Has anybody here gotten Perry Boston's autograph or shaken his hand or seen him open a door or eat anything?"

"C'mon, Joni—cut the guy some slack," Owen replied. "He's got a broken arm."

"Which one?"

"His right!" exclaimed Leslie with a burst of recognition.

"Correct," answered Joni. "A *left*-handed person with an injured *right* arm can still sign autographs. But Perry Boston told us he couldn't. I think he's just another hologram."

A glum silence descended on the room. Owen finally spoke up. "Suppose you're right, Joni, then where's the real Perry Boston?"

"I don't know," Joni said. "But Nogudnik did manage to take Perry Boston prisoner once before. Maybe he's done it again." She paused and held up Santiago's map. "Now that we have this, though, I think I know how we can smoke Nogudnik out."

"What's your idea?" Owen asked.

Joni winked. "Let's just say that tomorrow morning we're going to turn Boffo Pictures into Nogudnik's worst nightmare."

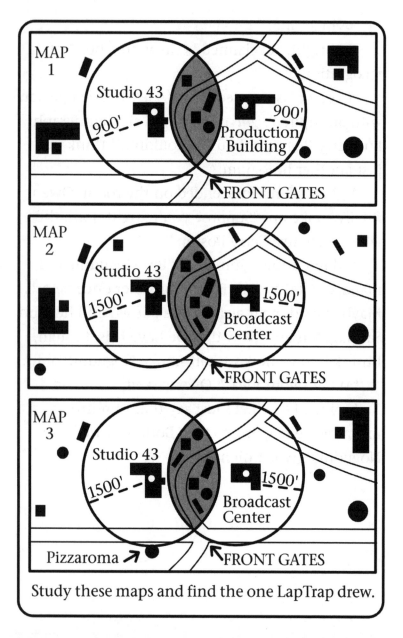

MAP 1

Studio 43

900'

900'

Production Building

FRONT GATES

MAP 2

Studio 43

1500'

1500'

Broadcast Center

FRONT GATES

MAP 3

Studio 43

1500'

1500'

Broadcast Center

Pizzaroma

FRONT GATES

Study these maps and find the one LapTrap drew.

MA_ON_AI_E PA_TI_S

"I sure hope nobody arrests us," LapTrap said apprehensively. It was before dawn on Tuesday morning. Santiago used a flashlight and LapTrap's auxiliary headlights for illumination as he hooked up the laptop's cables to the mainframe computers in the basement of Studio 43.

"Don't worry," Santiago said. "Joni cleared everything with Wilton Thumbling last night. All the guards know you're here and the systems control people are expecting things to go, well, a bit differently this morning."

"But I don't like being left alone in the cold and the dark."

"It'll only be for a few hours," Santiago said. "Remember, you're the key to this whole operation. You'll be in charge of every sign, message board, and closed-circuit TV on the lot. And don't forget, Owen's patrolling the grounds on his skateboard. He's depending on you to report any strange activity in the yellow zone."

"Me, forget?" LapTrap said. "I've got a memory

bigger than the Grand Canyon."

Santiago glanced at his watch. "It's seven-fifty. I gotta run."

LapTrap squirmed. "Can't you stay a little longer?"

Santiago shook his head. "Joni and Leslie and Wilton Thumbling are waiting for me in the cafeteria. We're meeting Perry Boston for breakfast at eight. You know the plan."

LapTrap nodded yes. "But, Santiago... there's one more thing."

"Yes?"

"What should I do to keep from being lonely?"

Santiago smiled. "Why don't you rehearse the lines for your screen test?"

LapTrap's expression brightened. "Say, that's a terrific idea!"

As Santiago left the mainframe room, he could hear LapTrap speaking in a deep dramatic voice: *"The sit-u-ation's grim, Cap-tain Boom-bah. It looks like the e-vil mon-key king has jammed our quark fib-ril-la-tors again!"*

⊡⊡

At a few minutes past eight, Santiago hurried into

the Boffo cafeteria, a huge glass-domed building that looked as if it had been designed by an eccentric jungle explorer. Each table sat in the leafy shade of a giant Venus-flytrap. Chattering monkeys swung from tangled vines that crisscrossed the upper reaches of the dome. Tropical birds flew everywhere, and an iced-coffee waterfall tumbled over a twenty-foot-high "cliff" made entirely of petrified lima beans.

Santiago quickly located his friends. Joni and Leslie were seated with Wilton Thumbling, next to the biggest Venus-flytrap in the cafeteria. Perry Boston had not yet arrived.

"Good to see you, kid," Wilton Thumbling said as Santiago pulled up a chair. "You know," the director said to the group, "this is my favorite eating place. You never have to worry about bugs in your food. Gwendolyn here"—he patted the trunk of the Venus-flytrap—"just crunches 'em up. You got to watch her, though. She'll steal the meatloaf right off your plate."

"Er… how fascinating," said Leslie, glancing uneasily over her shoulder at Gwendolyn.

Joni's eyes were fixed on the entrance. "Here comes our man," she whispered as Perry Boston approached in a light jacket, his right arm still cradled in a sling.

"Morning, Perry," Wilton Thumbling said with a big grin. "Grab a chair and sit down."

Perry Boston smiled back nervously. "I wonder, Wilton, if you wouldn't mind fetching a chair for me. My right arm's still useless and now my left's sprained from overuse."

"Sorry to hear that, Perry," Wilton Thumbling said, signaling for a waiter to bring another chair over to the table. Perry Boston squeezed into it without too much trouble.

Wilton Thumbling rubbed his hands together hungrily. "Okay, what's everyone having? Breakfast's on me."

"Where's the menu?" Leslie asked.

"Oh, we don't use printed menus here," Wilton Thumbling explained. "Everything's on that electric sign—over there." He pointed to a large rotating panel in the center of the cafeteria. The breakfast selections were displayed in red lights. But something was amiss with the lettering.

```
BREAKFAST SELECTIONS (TUESDAY):

1. Or_n_e Ju_ce — 75¢          7. _ppl_ _uice — 75¢

2. P_une Ju_c_ — 75¢           8. G_ap_ Jui_ _ — 75¢

3. K_tch_p — Free              9. Bo_tl_d Wa_er — 90¢

4. Sc_ _mbled Eggs — $2.75    10. Tap _ _t_r — 35¢

5. H_m & _ggs — $3.06         11. Ma_on_ai_e Pa_ti_s — 43¢

6. Coff_e, T_a — 85¢          12. Sal_d Bar — $4.89
```

"Um, I'll try numbers 2 and 4—whatever they are," Leslie said.

"Numbers 5 and 11 look interesting," Joni said. "Do you eat them with a fork or a spoon?"

"Beats me," Wilton Thumbling replied. "Santiago?"

"I'm torn between 'Orne Juce'—is that how you pronounce it?—and number 12."

"Live it up, kid. Get 'em both," Wilton Thumbling said.

"Thanks, I will."

"And you, Perry?" Wilton Thumbling asked.

Perry Boston did not respond. His eyes were bulging, his teeth were clenched, and he was sweating profusely.

"Everything okay, Perry?" Wilton Thumbling inquired. "You look, well, unwell."

Perry Boston raised his right arm and covered his eyes.

"Hey, look, kids—it's a miracle!" Wilton Thumbling exclaimed. "Perry's arm got better."

"Don't mock me, Thumbling," Perry Boston said. "You know what's bothering me. Your menus are missing letters. Have you no shame? You are destroying civilization as we know it!"

"Must be a glitch in the mainframes in Studio 43," Wilton Thumbling remarked. "I'll have somebody fix it later."

Perry Boston jumped up, his eyes still covered. "No, I insist you fix it now."

"Sit down, Perry!" the director snapped. "We have unfinished business we need to discuss—like the banshee... the alien... and your efforts to destroy my movie and my hologram project."

"I—I don't know what you're talking about," Perry Boston spluttered.

"Oh, don't you?" Wilton Thumbling said. He picked up a cloth napkin. "Here, catch!" he said, tossing it at the standing figure. The object passed right through Perry Boston. The director turned to the ClueFinders. "Hey, you guys were right! He's nothing but a hologram."

The Perry Boston hologram dropped his arm and stared, trembling, at the rotating menu panel. "I can't stand this anymore!" he screamed. "Please, fix those words. Doesn't anybody care?"

Joni got up and looked the Perry Boston mirage squarely in the eye. "You can stop pretending, Nogudnik," she said. "We know you're controlling this hologram. And I know you can you see and hear me. Show yourself as you really are."

Slowly the hologram changed shape. The body grew dumpy, the face lengthened, the hair turned bristly, and the eyes acquired dark lines and bags.

"That's better," Joni said. "More like the real you."

"*Now* will you fix the menu?" the Nogudnik hologram whimpered.

Joni signaled to Leslie, who was on the videophone with LapTrap. "Tell LapTrap to fix half the words," she said.

Half the missing letters reappeared.

"Do the rest!" pleaded the Nogudnik hologram.

"First tell me where the real Perry Boston is," Joni said.

"He's my prisoner."

"Where?"

"With me—in my hideout."

"Where's that?"

"The rest! Fix the rest!"

Joni nodded to Leslie, who instructed LapTrap to fill in the remaining letters.

"Now, where's Perry Boston?" demanded Joni.

The Nogudnik hologram gazed at the restored words and relaxed. "That's for me to know and you to find out," he cackled, and dashed toward the iced-coffee waterfall.

"Stop him, Santiago!" Joni cried.

Santiago pulled out his photonic blocker. "There's nothing I hate worse than a hologram that plays dirty tricks on people," he said. He aimed the device at the hologram and called out, "Nogudnik— wherever you are—we're coming after you!"

As the hologram leaped into the iced-coffee falls, Santiago pressed ENTER. A dazzling pink corkscrew enveloped the hologram. It spun forward, crackled with electrostatic sparks, and burst like a soap bubble on the lima bean cliff.

"Neat trick!" Wilton Thumbling said. "I sure could use one of those when I'm holding auditions."

CAUTION

PLEASE STEP CAREFULY,
AS THERE ARE
ELECTRICLE WIRES
UNDERFOOT.
ALL ACTERS MUST BE
WEARING SHOES
NO EXEPTIONS!
ALSO, NO FOOD OR
BEVERIDGES ON THE SET.

PLEASE PAY STRICK
ATTENSION TO THESE
REGGULATIONS!

Circle and correct the misspelled words.

PYRAMID SCHEME

"Ready to execute Phase II, LapTrap?" Joni called into her videophone.

"Ready, Joni," LapTrap reported back.

"Okay, three… two… one… execute!"

All the computerized signs on the Boffo backlot momentarily went blank. When they blinked on again, every sign had scrambled or missing letters. NO LEFT TURN became FUNNEL TROT. BROADCAST CENTER was now BAD CONCRETE STAR. STAGE DOOR was replaced by ODORS GATE. NOW SHOOTING became NO_ _HOOTING.

Confusion broke out. Traffic became snarled on the roadways leading to Boffo buildings. Employees gathered outside buildings, wondering if someone was playing practical jokes. But soon the security guards got things back under control. Following Wilton Thumbling's instructions, they told the Boffo employees to ignore the malfunctioning signs and go about their work as usual.

Meanwhile, Joni, Leslie, and Santiago searched for Morris Nogudnik's hideout in the six buildings in Santiago's yellow zone. And Owen continued to prowl the grounds on his skateboard, on the lookout for anyone behaving suspiciously.

"Anything yet, guys?" Joni called into the videophone as the three teammates swept through separate floors of the scenery construction building. She could see Leslie and Santiago on the split screen.

"Negative," Santiago replied.

"Negative here, too," responded Leslie.

Suddenly the videoscreen split into thirds. Owen appeared.

"I'm approaching Studio 19, behind the first aid center," he said excitedly. "They're filming *The Mummy's Mommy* there. I see a dumpy guy in an Egyptian costume wearing heavy makeup and a turban. He just used a marker to change an APRON KING sign back to a NO PARKING sign."

"What's he doing now?"

"Correcting a misspelled word inside the AGE TRANCE."

"You mean, STAGE ENTRANCE?"

"Oh, right."

"That's our man!" Joni cried. "Go after him. We're on our way."

"Roger!" Owen said.

The four ClueFinders rendezvoused at the stage entrance to *The Mummy's Mommy* set. "You're sure he hasn't slipped by you?" Santiago asked Owen.

"Positive," Owen said. "I asked LapTrap to lock all the doors except this one. Nogudnik's definitely in there. You can't miss him. He's wearing a funky Egyptian outfit."

"Okay, guys, let's roll!" Joni ordered as the ClueFinders sprinted up a long ramp leading onto the *The Mummy's Mommy* soundstage.

A huge crowd of extras was swarming around the base of a not-quite-finished white plastic pyramid that stood about 150 feet high.

"Uh-oh! *Everybody's* dressed like an Egyptian," Leslie said in despair. "How are we going to find Nogudnik?"

"Look for somebody shielding his eyes," Joni said.

"What do you mean?" Owen asked.

"The Perry Boston hologram covered his eyes to avoid seeing the menu. He did that because that's what Nogudnik would do."

"I see dozens of people shielding their eyes,"

Leslie said. "The spotlights are intense."

"Have LapTrap lower them," Joni said.

Seconds later, the lights in Studio 19 dimmed. Only one man remained with his hand over his eyes.

"That's him!" cried Owen. "I recognize his headgear."

The ClueFinders charged into the crowd. Hearing the commotion, Morris Nogudnik glanced up briefly and spotted the ClueFinders. There was only one place for him to go. In terror, he clambered up one side of the plastic pyramid.

"Leslie, you take the north face," Joni directed. "Owen, the south. Santiago, the east. I'll take the west. Let's force him to the top."

"But I hate heights!" cried Santiago.

"Don't look down and you'll be fine!" Owen encouraged.

"Easy for you to say," Santiago retorted.

Morris Nogudnik tied up the end of his long, flowing robe so that he could ascend faster. Even so, he stumbled with every row he climbed. The top of the pyramid was adorned with colorful pictures and inscriptions, written in ancient Egyptian hieroglyphics. Near the top, a small door used by the set designers opened into the plastic structure.

"Don't let him reach the door!" Joni yelled out. "He might escape down inside."

Morris Nogudnik hurled himself higher and higher. But Owen and Joni, the most athletic of the ClueFinders, were gaining on him.

"Give up, Morris!" Joni called out. "Your hologram-making days are over."

"You'll have to catch me first, ClueFinders! And there are no electric signs up here to stop me."

Joni gazed upwards. Morris Nogudnik was only two rows from the door. Owen scooted over to Joni's side. "We're not going to get him unless I pour on the juice," he whispered to Joni. With a grunt, Owen pulled himself up to within one row of Nogudnik.

As Morris Nogudnik swung a leg through the open door, Owen jumped and caught the knotted end of Nogudnik's gown. Nogudnik scowled and shook himself free. "So long, ClueFind—" he began.

Then he froze. It was all the time Owen needed. He leaped onto the next row, pulled Nogudnik's leg back outside, and slammed the pyramid door.

When Joni reached the top, Owen had

everything under control. He'd tied Morris Nogudnik's hands together with a sash from the gown. But, strangely, Morris Nogudnik was behaving as meekly as a mouse.

"I don't get it, Joni," Owen said, looking perplexed. "Nogudnik shook me off and was about to make a getaway, but then he stopped. Now look at him."

Morris Nogudnik sniveled and sobbed. "I lost my marker. I need my marker. Please help me."

"Help you do what, dude?"

"These hieroglyphics—they're painted wrong… someone misspelled them! I need to correct them."

Joni and Owen exchanged glances and burst out laughing. "Who knew he could read ancient Egyptian?" Joni said.

An hour later, after the police took custody of Morris Nogudnik, the ClueFinders freed the real Perry Boston from Nogudnik's hideout in the boiler room in Building M. There they also found Morris Nogudnik's 3-D hologram projector, which they agreed they would turn over to the National Museum for the Advancement of Cool Ideas.

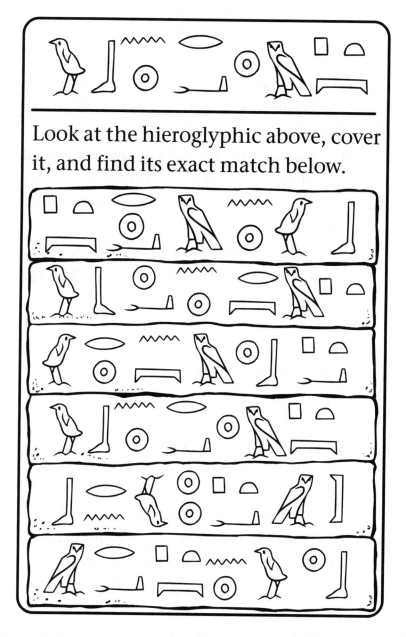

Look at the hieroglyphic above, cover it, and find its exact match below.

EPILOGUE

The ClueFinders and a grateful Perry Boston all went to watch LapTrap's screen test for Lulu Randango's new sci-fi thriller, *The Attack of the 90-Foot Android Sisters*.

"My dar-ling little tin cup," Lulu Randango said as LapTrap flew in the door with his friends. "Please take a seat on the audition bench—or flut-ter in the air above, if you'd like."

"How do my corners and planes look today?" LapTrap said, twisting this way and that. "Santiago gave me a good polishing."

"Delicious, dar-ling, now you join the others on the audition bench."

"Others?" said LapTrap.

"Why, of course, butter-cup. This is Holly-wood." She pivoted on her stiletto heels and scurried back to her director's chair.

"Looks like you've got a lot of company," Santiago said, gazing toward the bench.

LapTrap rotated and saw an assortment of laptops, droids, motorized battlebots, and radio-controlled kids' toys sitting in the waiting area. Some were reading the newspaper, others were joking or playing cards; still others were nervously chewing their fingernails, if they had them.

LapTrap gulped. "Hey, I thought this was going to be *my* audition."

"That's what we all thought," one laser-guided cheese slicer said.

Two hours later, LapTrap was called into a small room with a curtain, a camera, a stool, and several spotlights. Lulu and her assistant were seated in lounge chairs behind the camera.

"Do you want to see my profile?" LapTrap asked.

"I want to see *you* as *you* see yourself as you," Lulu replied.

"Okay," LapTrap said. He flipped his lid to display his screen and lengthy program menu.

"Ex-cellent, my little whirligig," Lulu Randango said. "I will now give you Cap-tain Boom-bah's line, and you will recite your part. Ready?"

"R-r-ready," said LapTrap, tensely clearing his throat.

"*What is the intergalactic situation report, Droidle-2C?*" Lulu Randango recited.

"*The sit-u-ation's grim, Cap-tain Boom-bah,*" LapTrap responded, flexing his eyebrows. "*It looks like the e-vil mon-key king has jammed our quark fib-*

ril-la-tors again!"

"Per-fect!" Lulu Randango said with a smile. "Now toddle on."

"Toddle on?"

"Yes, my purple push-kin—leave. I must confer with my assistant, Jules."

"I'm yellow."

"Yellow-shmellow. Purple is a form of yellow."

"B-but, do I get the part?" LapTrap asked hesitantly.

Lulu Randango and her assistant whispered together. Then Lulu Randango rose from her lounge chair and stroked LapTrap above his eyebrows. "You were brilliant, sim-ply brilliant," she said. "But Jules feels, and I must agree, that we need someone— how should I say it?—a bit younger and a little less yellow."

"W-what?" stammered LapTrap, crestfallen. "But you said—"

"I never say what I say, my lit-tle radish. Next!"

A three-speed vacuum cleaner rolled into the room and brushed LapTrap off his stool.

"Ready, my precious rug snurf-ler," Lulu said.

LapTrap rejoined the ClueFinders with a sad look in his eyes. Joni slipped an arm around his case.

"Sorry it didn't go as you'd hoped," she said. "But, you know, we would have hated to lose you to Hollywood."

"Yeah, little buddy," said Santiago. "You're irreplaceable."

Perry Boston stepped forward. "Hey, LapTrap," he said with a wink, "you're not the only one who's had a disappointing Hollywood experience. Mine hasn't been exactly a picnic. But if it hadn't been for your courage and good work, I'd still be Morris Nogudnik's prisoner." Then he popped LapTrap's lid, took out a light pen, and—with his left hand— wrote the following on LapTrap's screen:

"To my dear friend LapTrap and his friends, the ClueFinders: Words cannot express how much I owe you. When it comes to solving mysteries no one is better than you five."

He said, "Maybe you can scan that onto your hard disk for safe-keeping." Then he snapped LapTrap's lid shut.

"Thanks, Mr. Boston!" LapTrap beamed.

Joni's blue eyes twinkled. She said, "Now we can say that this case and LapTrap's are both closed."

Looking for the answers to the puzzles? Here they are!

Chapter 1

Flip Your Wig is closest.

Chapter 2

1. star, 2. SF, 3. tufts,
4. Thumbling, 5. Clue,
6. double, 7. Savage

Chapter 3

It's the lower-left alien.

Chapter 4

Have fun drawing!

Chapter 5

Fish: anchovies, herring, tuna. Four syllables: asparagus, huckleberries, pepperoni, rutabaga. Verbs: mint, squash. Fungus: mushroom.

Chapter 6

1. MOVIE, 2. ACTOR,
3. LINES, 4, THEATER,
5. CAMERA, 6. MAKEUP

Chapter 7

LapTrap drew the map in the middle.

Chapter 8

CAREFULLY, ELECTRICAL, ACTORS, EXCEPTIONS, BEVERAGES, STRICT, ATTENTION, REGULATIONS

Chapter 9

The correct hieroglyphic is third up from the bottom.